Hanukkah vs. Santa Claus

Written by David Michael Slater

Illustrated by Michelle Simpson

Published by:
Library Tales Publishing
www.LibraryTalesPublishing.com
www.Facebook.com/LibraryTalesPublishing

Copyright © 2017 by David Michael Slater
Published by Library Tales Publishing, Inc., New York, New York

For general information on our other products and services, please contact our Customer Care Department at 1-800-754-5016, or fax 917-463-0892. For technical support, please visit www.LibraryTalesPublishing.com

Library Tales Publishing also publishes its books in a variety of electronic formats. Every content that appears in print is available in electronic books.

** PRINTED IN THE UNITED STATES OF AMERICA **

ISBN-13:978-0999275825
ISBN-10: 0999275828

LIBRARY TALES PUBLISHING

For Hanukkah Harvey Slater – Dms

Hanukkah Harvie
vs. Santa Claus

The Chrismukkah Kerfuffle

Written by David Michael Slater
Illustrated by Michelle Simpson

The moment Harvie woke up,
he got things in gear.

Hanukkah started tonight!

It was a good thing preparing
the oil helped him limber up.

Delivering eight night's worth
of gifts at one time was a serious shlep!

The workshop was running like a well-oiled machine.

It was almost sundown.
Time to heat up the Hanukkopter.

Harvie waited for the first star, then took off.

Harvie landed at his first home.

The family was noshing on latkes and jelly donuts and playing dreidel. **Hanukkool**, Harvie thought.

Harvie chose some oil, then sprinkled it about.
Then he did his thing.

Hanukkawesome, Harvie thought, perfectly placing his final present. Things were going like clockwork.

But then something happened that had never happened before.
As Harvie was quietly backing away, he bumped into someone.
Santa Claus!
It was also Christmas Eve!

Harvie looked at the gifts
Santa left under the tree.

Santa looked at the gifts Harvie
left next to the menorah.

They shook hands and smiled...
while they both slipped an extra
present onto their piles.

They scowled.
Then they both slipped another
present onto their piles.

Harvie made quick work of houses
that only had menorahs.

Santa made quick work of houses
that only had trees.

But when they found
houses with both...

It. Was. ON!
It was on all over the world.

There were lots of houses with both.

Lots and lots of houses with both!

Who knows what would have happened if Hanukkah Harvie and Santa Claus hadn't arrived together at the very last house.

"You two are silly," someone said.
"Who said that?" Harvie hollered.
"Who's there?" Santa snapped.
"Me!" said a little voice.

And then they saw her.

"We're not silly!"
Santa and Harvie insisted.

"I just want to make sure you like Hanukkah better!"
Harvie explained.

"I just want to make sure you like Christmas better!"
Santa explained.

"But we don't have Hanukkah," the little girl told them.
"And we don't have Christmas, either."

"Right!" said the little girl.

"We have Christmukkah!"

"Wonderful!"
Harvie and Santa declared.

And from that moment on,
Harvie delivered gifts to the Hanukkah homes,
and Santa delivered gifts to the Christmas homes.

But they delivered Christmukkah presents **together.**

ABOUT THE AUTHOR

David Michael Slater is an acclaimed author of over 20 books for children, teens, and adults. His work for children includes the picture books *Cheese Louise!*, *The Bored Book*, and *The Boy & the Book*; the early chapter book series *Mysterious Monsters*; and the teen series *Forbidden Books*. David's work for adults includes *We're Doing It Wrong: 25 Ideas in Education That Just Don't Work — And How to Fix Them* and the novel *Fun & Games*, which the New York Journal of Books called "hilarious." David teaches in Reno, Nevada, where he lives with his wife and son. You can learn more about David and his work at **www.davidmichaelslater.com.**

ABOUT THE ILLUSTRATOR

Michelle Simpson graduated from Sheridan College with a BAA in Illustration in 2014 and has been working as an illustrator since. Her self-published children's book, *Monsters In My House*, won the Brenda Clark book prize award. It was also short-listed for the Canadian Self-Publishing awards. Michelle runs her own online shop where she sells lots of cute fantastical illustrated items. To buy or view more of her illustrated work visit her online.

Shop at: www.michiscribbles.etsy.com

Portfolio: www.michellescribbles.com

Made in the USA
Las Vegas, NV
05 April 2023